To my daddy, whose stories about the preachán and the bodach were the best, and to Martha for changing my life, with love—A. M.

To Marion and the magnificent Milroys, with love—R. B.

2010 First U.S. edition
Text copyright © 2010 by Anna McQuinn
Illustrations copyright © 2009, 2010 by Rosalind Beardshaw

Published by Charlesbridge
85 Main Street
Watertown, MA 02472
(617) 926-0329
www.charlesbridge.com

First published in the United Kingdom in 2009 by Alanna Books,
46 Chalvey Road East, Slough, Berkshire, SL1 2LR, United Kingdom,
as *Lulu Loves Stories*. Copyright © 2009 Alanna Books
www.alannabooks.com

Library of Congress Cataloging-in-Publication Data
McQuinn, Anna.
    Lola loves stories / Anna McQuinn ; illustrated by Rosalind Beardshaw.
        p. cm.
    Summary: Lola loves to hear Daddy read a new library book each night, an activity
that spurs her imagination and results in inventive play the next day.
    ISBN 978-1-58089-258-2 (reinforced for library use)
    ISBN 978-1-58089-259-9 (softcover)
[1. Books and reading—Fiction. 2. Imagination—Fiction. 3. African
Americans—Fiction.] I. Beardshaw, Rosalind, ill. II. Title.
PZ7.M47883Lq 2010
[E]—dc22   2009026885

Printed in China
(hc) 10 9 8 7 6 5 4 3 2 1
(sc) 10 9 8 7 6 5 4 3 2 1

Illustrations done in acrylic on paper
Display type and text type set in Garamouche Bold and Billy
Color separations by Chroma Graphics, Singapore
Manufactured by Regent Publishing Services, Hong Kong
Printed February 2010 in ShenZhen, Guangdong, China
Production supervision by Brian G. Walker
Designed by Martha MacLeod Sikkema

Lola Loves Stories

Anna McQuinn

Illustrated by Rosalind Beardshaw

iꟾꞛꞛi Charlesbridge

Lola's daddy takes her to the library on Saturdays.

The library is *very* busy,

but Lola finds some excellent books.

Lola's daddy reads the
first story at home.
It is about a
fairy princess.

All the next day
Lola wears a fancy dress
and a sparkly crown.
She is a fabulous fairy princess!

On Sunday night Lola and her mommy read the next story. It is about an amazing journey.

On Monday Lola takes her friends on fantastic trips to places like Paris and Lagos.

On Tuesday Lola chooses a story
about friends.

All afternoon she and Ben play with their babies. Lola has cappuccino, and her baby has juice.

Tuesday night Lola's mommy reads a story about fierce tigers.

The next day Lola chases her friend
Orla all over the jungle.

On Wednesday night Lola reads
a story about Old MacDonald.
The next day she is a farmer.
Lola's cow has a boo-boo!

Mommy knows how to fix it.

On Thursday night Lola and her daddy read about building.

The next day Lola fixes up her house.
She needs a hammer, a saw . . .
and a little help from her daddy.

On Friday night Lola's daddy makes up a story about magic shoes. The next day Lola's shoes are truly amazing.

They sparkle all the way to the library . . .

. . . and all the way home.

They even sparkle while her daddy reads her a story about a wild and wicked monster!

What will Lola be tomorrow?